THE HUNGRY BABY BUNNY

By ALF EVERS

Pictures by BEA RABIN SEIDEN

WONDER BOOKS • **NEW YORK**
A Division of GROSSET & DUNLAP, Inc.

THE BABY BUNNY had two long ears. He had two pink
eyes, one pink nose, a little button mouth and four hoppity
legs. His fur was soft as silk from the tip of his pink nose to
the tip of his funny little cotton tail.

The Baby Bunny lived in a little green house of his own
on a farm. There was a fence all around the house.

The Baby Bunny could do a great many little things.
He could jump!

He could wiggle his ears.

He could wiggle his nose.

He could even wiggle his ears and nose at the same time!

But he had never done anything really important, and he wanted to.

Then one day the farmer forgot to feed the Baby Bunny.

Late at night the Baby Bunny woke up.

He was hungry — and *very* angry.

He dug a hole under the fence around his little house and
wriggled out.

Then he went straight to the field of lettuce across the road.

He felt hungry enough to eat every head of lettuce there. He sat down and started to eat.

The Baby Bunny knew that the farmer didn't want him to eat the lettuce.

Even the wild bunnies in the woods knew that. But the Baby Bunny thought that the farmer wouldn't mind if he ate a little.

He was *so* hungry.

Pretty soon he heard a little noise.

He saw a wild bunny sniffing at the lettuce. The wild bunny was hungry, too.

When the wild bunny saw the Baby Bunny eating, he thought that it would be all right to eat some lettuce himself.

So he sat down and ate and ate.

Soon the Baby Bunny heard another little noise. A second

wild bunny came up. When he saw the two bunnies eating, he started to eat the lettuce, too.

Then another bunny came, and then another — and another — young bunnies, old bunnies and little wild bunnies. The whole field was just full of bunnies.

All of them were eating lettuce as fast as they could. And they ate and ate and ate!

After a while the sun came up. All the wild bunnies scam-
pered home to the woods.

There was only one single piece of lettuce left in the field.
It was the last bit of the head of lettuce the Baby Bunny was
nibbling.

He took much longer to eat than the wild bunnies, because he ate much more nicely.

Soon the Baby Bunny heard a rattling and scraping sort of noise. The farmer was coming with his horse and plow.

When the farmer looked at the lettuce field, he just rubbed his eyes.

Then he stared at the field again.

All the lettuce was gone except for one tiny piece.

And the Baby Bunny had almost finished that.

The farmer *should* have been angry. But he was sorry that he had forgotten to feed the Baby Bunny the night before.

He was so surprised at seeing the lettuce gone that he shouted:

"Wonderful, wonderful! It serves me right. The Baby Bunny has eaten my whole field of lettuce."

Away he ran to tell everyone he knew all about it, and everyone he told came to see for himself what Baby Bunny had done. But Baby Bunny left before anyone came.

He didn't see the men, women and children, cows and pigs, cats, geese and chickens, all staring at the field, saying: "Wonderful, just wonderful!"

He just walked straight home, lay down and went to sleep.

Every day people and animals came to look at the Baby Bunny.

All of them thought that the Baby Bunny had eaten a whole field of lettuce in one night. They thought the Baby Bunny was wonderful.

The farmer looked at the Baby Bunny, too. He said, "The Baby Bunny is wonderful. He ate a whole field of lettuce in one night. But I don't want that to happen again. I'll feed the Baby Bunny on time. And I'll feed him so well that he will never want to eat the lettuce in my fields again."

Then the farmer gave the Baby Bunny a big basket of fresh carrots to eat. The Baby Bunny jumped and wiggled his ears with happiness. He was happy to have the carrots. But he was even happier because he had taught the farmer never, never to forget to feed him again. And that was a pretty important thing for a Baby Bunny to do.